GIMME, GIMME
Moocher Marmots

Written and
Illustrated by
Cindy Burchfield

First published by Dog Ear Publishing
4010 W. 86th Street, Ste H
Indianapolis, IN 46268
www.dogearpublishing.net

ISBN: 978-159858-457-8

This book is printed on acid-free paper.

Printed in the United States of America

For Kevin, Sara and Jamie

Juli
Donna
Alvin
John
Jason
Aaron
Aimee
Chad
Chris
Dustin
Marty
Kenny
Hoot
Zac
Monty
Jill
Jim
&
Sam

GIMME, GIMME
Moocher Marmots

I confess I fed the varmints
and to this day I'll not forget
the price I had to pay for it.

Moocher Marmots arrive each spring.
Their alarms after months do ring.
From a sleepy state they wake
desiring just a smidge of cake.

For Moocher Marmots are unique.
"We don't care for grass," they squeak,
"We prefer things in wrappers
often shared by friendly campers."

Innocently I gave to one
a small morsel. It seemed a crumb.

Okay, okay!
I must come clean.
It was a lime green jelly bean.

But who'd have guessed what was in store.
Up popped the faces of two more.

From the bushes they ran toward me.
Their squeals resounding, "Gimme, gimme!"

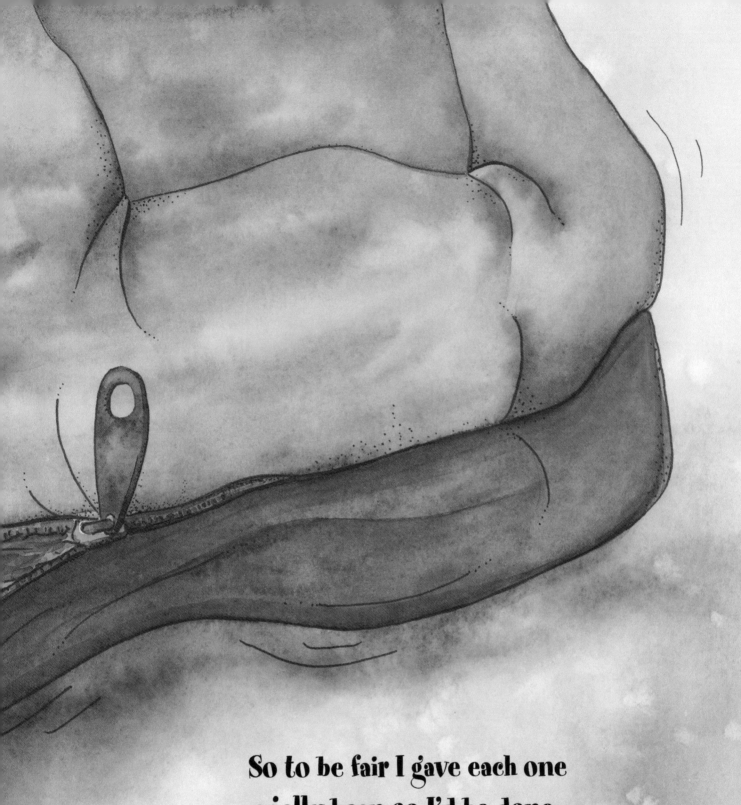

So to be fair I gave each one
a jelly bean so I'd be done.
Then while my head was turned
the first into my backpack wormed.

Before I could capture it,
he'd left me with but one peach pit.
Again I tried to shoo the others
and turned to find just bowls and covers.

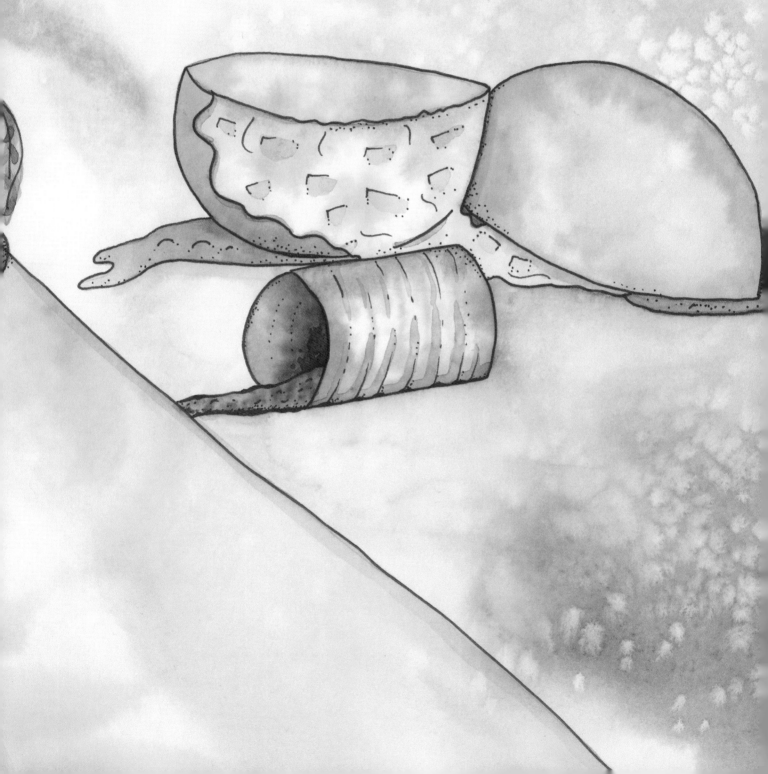

Cookies, chips, crackers, candy
to Moocher Marmots all were dandy.
With such delight their tummies roared,
"Tasty, creamy, gooey s'mores!"

"Gimme, gimme," Moocher Marmots chirped
as one leaned back and loudly burped.

Just when I thought they were done
one asked me for a hot dog bun.

I know marmots don't eat meat.

"For Moocher Marmots
it's a treat!"

Into my cooler they did dive
and not a wiener would survive.

For my tent I did flee.
Eat all you want, but please spare me!

When they'd finished my last day's grub,
they spied my car and said, "Yum, yum!"

Hiding deep within my tent,
I gasped at the Moochers' intent.
Surely not a car they'd eat.

**"For Moocher Marmots
it's a treat!"**

My seats, my top, all that was edible -
now I'm the proud owner of a Marmot Convertible.
"Crunch, munch, crunch," they went all night.
Would nothing stop their appetite?

Nothing left by dawn next morning,
but myself and this warning.

Unsuspecting campers near
were unaware of what to fear.
I screamed a warning down the lane.

I screamed a warning though in vain.

Don't feed the Marmots!

Don't be Dumb!

"What's the harm?
It's just a crumb."

THE
END

Gimme, Gimme Moocher Marmots is based on the journals of Sara and Jamie Caraker who first encountered the "Moocher Marmots" while camping with their aunt and uncle.

Marmots flourish throughout the national parks of the Western United States, Alaska, and can be found worldwide.

No marmots or jelly beans were harmed in the making of this story.

Cindy Burchfield is lost in Alaska. Since arriving on the shores of Southeast Alaska, Cindy has never looked back. She has a passion for the Alaskan lifestyle. She and her husband, a fishing guide, live it to the fullest. The imagery and icons of her travels in the Western U.S. and Alaska are captured in her watercolors and stories.

Cindy is an avid outdoorsman -- fishing, hunting, hiking and exploring the Last Frontier. She has hoisted a 214-pound halibut from a depth of 225 feet, landed and netted two salmon simultaneously and hunted remote beaches from her friend's Cessna 180.
She is undeniably Alaskan.

Cindy began painting as a child with her grandmother Juli Wilson, an accomplished oil painter. It was watercolors that landed Cindy in her first museum show at fourteen in Oklahoma City. An artist was born. Under the direction of her college professor, Arni Anderson, Cindy produced a considerable portfolio of watercolor work, most of which sold before graduation. A businesswoman was born.

Her talent for the written word as well as the visual arts landed Cindy in the field of marketing. She is also a member of the Juneau Artists Gallery, a local art cooperative. Lost in Alaska Studios is Cindy's home that she shares with her husband Kevin, Moose the Lab and Whiskey the Scottie, located high upon Marmot Bluff on North Douglas Island just across the channel from Juneau, Alaska.

Lost In Alaska Studios
lostinalaskastudios.com
lostinalaska@gci.net

Special thanks to:
David W. Riccio, www.lemoncreekdigital.com
Terra Parker, End of the Roll Photographics

My Camping Journal

Happy Camper:

Who I traveled with:

When we went:

Where we visited:

What we saw:

Who we met:

What I learned:

My Camping Journal

Happy Camper:

Who I traveled with:

When we went:

Where we visited:

What we saw:

Who we met:

What I learned:

My Camping Journal

Happy Camper:

Who I traveled with:

When we went:

Where we visited:

What we saw:

Who we met:

What I learned:

My Camping Journal

Happy Camper:

Who I traveled with:

When we went:

Where we visited:

What we saw:

Who we met:

What I learned:

My Camping Journal

Happy Camper:

Who I traveled with:

When we went:

Where we visited:

What we saw:

Who we met:

What I learned:

My Camping Journal

Happy Camper:

Who I traveled with:

When we went:

Where we visited:

What we saw:

Who we met:

What I learned:

My Camping Journal

Happy Camper:

Who I traveled with:

When we went:

Where we visited:

What we saw:

Who we met:

What I learned:

My Camping Journal

Happy Camper:

Who I traveled with:

When we went:

Where we visited:

What we saw:

Who we met:

What I learned:

Printed in the United States
98780LV00001B